THE LAST BASSELOPE

ONE FEROCIOUS STORY

Berkeley Breathed

Little, Brown and Company
New York Boston

For Pop, who starred in his own stories

Notes on the use of this book:
Not suggested for use by adults unless accompanied by a kid or a kid guardian.
No chewing on the pages.
The actual consumption of dandelions may cause warts.
Best results will be obtained when read in an open, sunny meadow or late at night under the covers with a flashlight. Under *no* conditions should a television be in the vicinity.

Little, Brown and Company

Time Warner Book Group
1271 Avenue of the Americas, New York, NY 10020
Visit our Web site at www.lb-kids.com

First Paperback Edition

ISBN 0-316-10761-1 (hc) / ISBN 0-316-12664-0 (pb)

LCCN 92-14467

HC: 10 9 8 7 6 5 4 3
PB: 10 9 8 7 6 5 4 3

SC

Manufactured in China

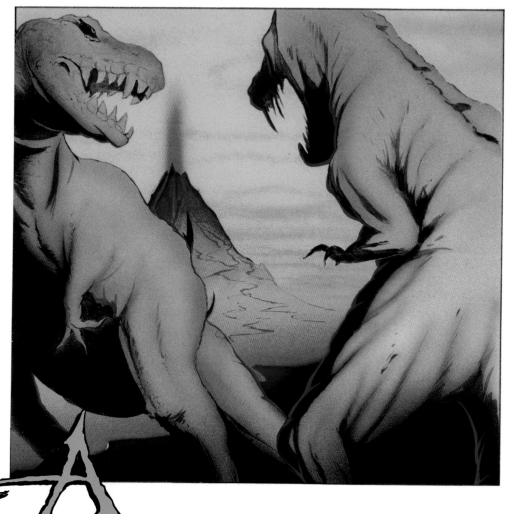

A very, terribly long time ago, before such things as television and good table manners or even children, ferocious monsters roamed a younger, angrier world.

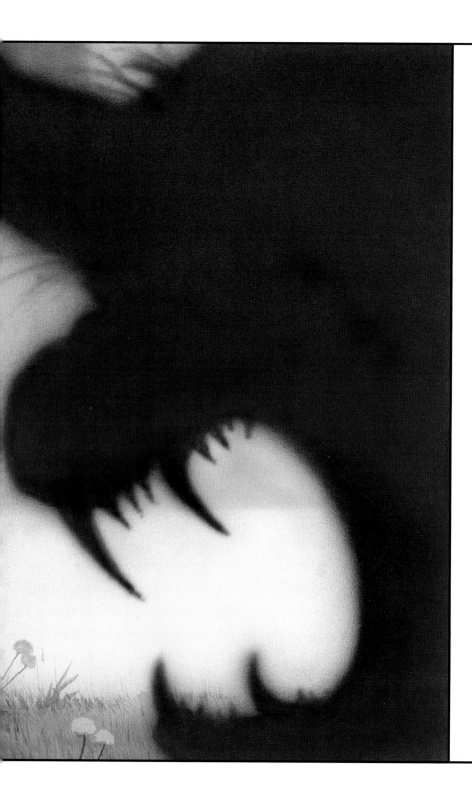

Whispered legends tell of a race of razor-horned, slobbery-fanged beasts more ferocious than the others. The stories say that the mere sight of one of them in a dinosaur neighborhood would inspire ripsnorting dinosaur pandemonium lasting for weeks.

Stories also say that a few of these brutes survived those terrible times. They say that just beyond our backyards, deep within the forest gloom, the very *last* one of them is still hiding, snarling, eating grizzly bears whole, and waiting to be discovered. They call him the Last Basselope.

Nobody read these basselope stories more closely than a Great and Famous Discoverer named Opus. Now, in truth, Opus was neither Great nor Famous and had discovered precisely *no* spotted tigers, *no* people-eating toads, and generally *no* lost tribes of Nebraskan cannibals. Even this morning, he couldn't discover two clean socks.

But he was hopeful. Surely, he thought, a Great and Famous Discoverer such as himself would soon discover *something*. And a razor-horned, slobbery-fanged basselope seemed a properly ferocious something. An expedition must be formed.

Opus found his best friends, Bill the Housecat, Milquetoast the Housebug, and Ronald-Ann the Housekid, watching TV in his living room — several TVs, actually. Opus flung open the front door and pointed out into the sunshine.

"The Great Basselope Expedition is forming outside!" he announced. "Ferocious things are still out there! Undiscovered things! Wonderful things!"

Ronald-Ann pointed out that there was a commercial for Tidy-Nose allergy spray on TV, which seemed wonderful enough, thank you.

"Volunteers, please. Form an orderly line outside. No pushing," ordered the Expedition Leader.

But they didn't form any line whatsoever, so he had to drag each of the volunteers out — Ronald-Ann twice. By the feet.

When Opus finally explained that they would all get on TV once the basselope was captured, attitudes improved. He assigned responsibilities to each of the expedition members: Bill the Cat would carry the survival gear, Milquetoast would watch for elephants and act as manager once they got famous, and Ronald-Ann would prepare the marshmallow/Gummy Bear milkshakes.

Bill discovered some scraps of cardboard and an old set of cow horns in some nearby trash and danced around like a basselope, amusing all but the Expedition Leader. Bill was scolded for goofing off and felt thoroughly useless.

"We're off!" announced Opus, and, with a mail-order basselope net in hand, he led the group out the back gate and down toward the massive trees beyond.

HMM!

They walked deep into the gloom of the ancient forest for many, many miles. The air was deathly still except for the unseen wings of unseen things gliding through the creeping mist. The Great Basselope Expeditionary Force was lost. Then, at their feet, they suddenly noticed an endless glowing carpet of dandelion puffs stretching in all directions. Stranger still, a mysterious path had been cut through this miniature white forest. Opus bent down for a closer look.

"The dandelion tops," he whispered, "have been whacked *clean* off!"

"Whacked!?" shrieked Ronald-Ann, horrified.

"Clean off," repeated Opus.

"By razor-sharp horns," guessed Milquetoast.

"The basselope has been through here," said the Expedition Leader nervously.

They followed the dandelion path into the distance.

That evening in camp, nobody really enjoyed their marshmallow/Gummy Bear/catsup milkshakes. It's never easy enjoying a good meal if one expects to be eaten soon oneself. Opus tucked Ronald-Ann under her blanket and then settled himself in. Bill stood guard in his underwear and tried to feel useful. Milquetoast put some cold cream on his face and retired, only to jump up, hollering that there was a bug under his blanket. He calmed down when Opus pointed out that it was just himself.

In the flickering firelight, Opus thought he saw horrible basselope shapes lurking nearby. He inched his hand out from under the blanket and held a deadly weapon at the ready. It was a long time before he fell asleep.

Opus awoke in the morning when a single tiny dandelion wisp landed gently on his nose, making him sneeze. The others awoke to find more of the little white tufts floating from the direction of a strange glow just beyond view.

Sleepily, they dressed and crept toward the edge of a deep clearing. Peering into the light, they didn't notice the other creatures of the forest, frozen in fear, gazing at the sight below.

"Look," whispered Opus.

Ronald-Ann held her breath. Bill hid his face. Milquetoast ran in the opposite direction, screaming.

Opus tiptoed closer. A single shaft of morning sun pierced the thick forest canopy and fell square upon a shining grassy meadow.

In the middle stood the fierce, the terrible, the Last Basselope.

Opus did not see any slobbery fangs, nor did he see any razor horns. In fact, the beast seemed to be humming. And he certainly wasn't eating grizzly bears whole. He was nibbling off the tops of dandelions.

"Nibbling?" Opus sputtered. "This isn't what I call *ferocious!*"

The basselope looked up. His nose began to quiver. Both lips curled up into a horrible snarl revealing rows of dripping teeth.

The monster began to lumber toward them.

"Uh-oh," said the Great but Not Especially Brave Discoverer.

"Retreat! Fall back! Backpedal!" commanded Opus. The entire Basselope Expeditionary Force went into full-throttle, no brakes, darn-the-torpedoes *reverse!*

They shot out into a huge open meadow, the spitting, snorting creature following close behind. Opus collapsed, exhausted, on the other side and found himself cowering under a massive shadow of dripping teeth and quivering basselope lips. How embarrassing, he thought, for a Famous Discoverer to die as a basselope snack.

The jaws gaped! The monster drew in his lungs for a final, dandelion-filled breath, and then…

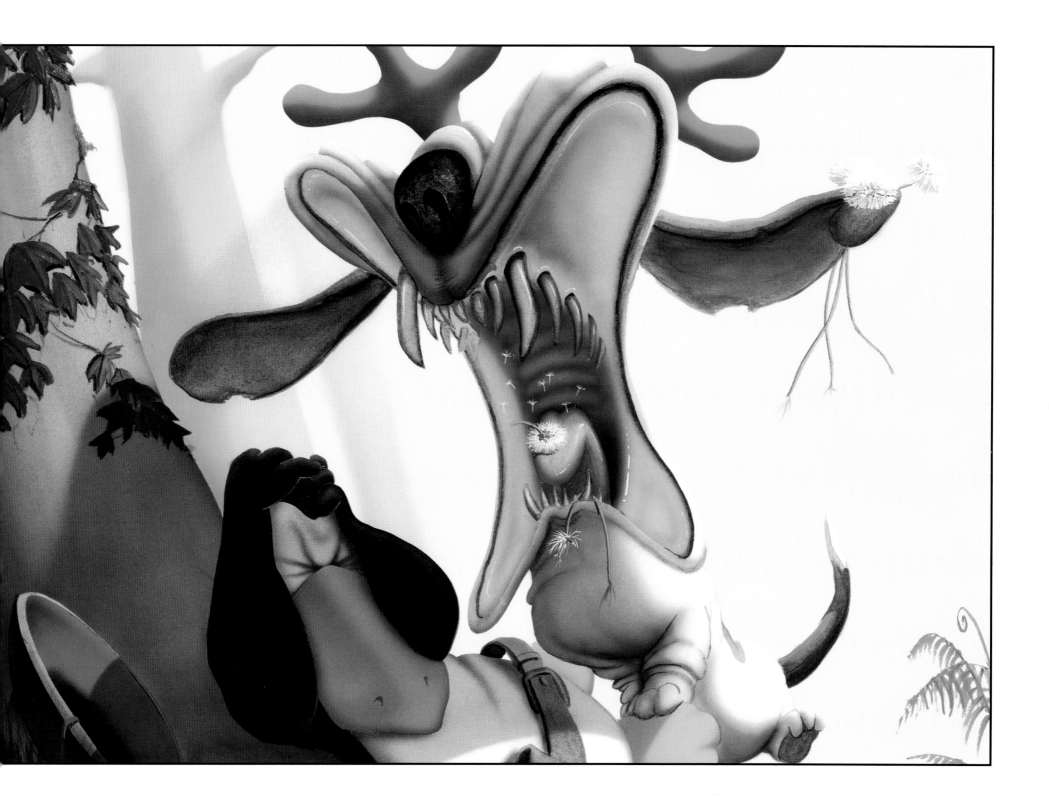

…he sneezed.

Oh, not a *normal* sneeze, not a run-of-the-mill, namby-pamby, plain-Jane, everyday reverse sniffle like yours or mine. No, *this* was a ten-megaton bull moose nasal explosion, propelling the creature backward in a graceful arc through the sky. With a plop, the basselope landed neatly on his bottom, very much as though he'd had some practice at all of this.

Snuffling, the basselope reached down with one of his huge ears and grasped a leaf, with which he blew his nose.

"Gesundheit," the beast said. "T'ank you," he replied to himself. He smiled shyly at the Expedition members and massaged his stuffy nose. "Dandelions always do dat to basselopes," he said. "We really shouldn't eat dem. But we *do* love dem so."

The Great Basselope Expeditionary Force cautiously walked over to the sniffling creature.

"The Last Basselope, I presume?" asked Opus, as formally as he could. The beast lifted his right ear and held it out to shake.

"Personal acquaintances call me Rosebud," he said. "At least dey would if I had any," the creature added with a sigh. "We basselopes hab been trying to make some for, oh, two hundred million years, but we'b neber been bery good at it." Then Rosebud grasped a dandelion stalk with an ear and inhaled the wisps with a snort. Again his lips began to curl and his nose wrinkled into a ferocious sneer. Opus shrank back in horror. Bill covered his eyes.

But Ronald-Ann pulled out a small spray bottle from her pocket. She squirted the stuff into the basselope's twitching, snarling honker, which then immediately unsnarled. The bottle read: TIDY-NOSE ALLERGY SPRAY.

PHOOT!

"Maybe personal acquaintances will be easier to make now," said Ronald-Ann, smiling. "You can start with us." And to celebrate, they spent the rest of the day collecting huge numbers of dandelions for a grand feast. Actually, only Rosebud did the eating. The others jumped into the pile.

TIDY-NOSE Allergy Spray

Suddenly Rosebud pricked up his ears. A noise came from deep within the forest, a noise unlike any he'd heard before. Everyone turned to look.

An avalanche of honking, roaring, squealing cars and trucks burst from the forest. Written across their sides were the names of TV shows and satellite networks and newspapers and magazines and animal zoos and tour companies.

And there, hanging on to the hood ornament of the lead vehicle, was former Expedition Member Milquetoast the Housebug, pointing the way. "We've got him cornered!" he hollered. "Bring him back alive!"

Rosebud turned to Opus. "More acquaintances?" he asked hopefully.

"Many, many more," said Opus, looking worried. He thought for a second and then turned to Bill. "We have to work fast," he said to the cat.

The parade of cars and trucks roared across the meadow. They surrounded the Great Basselope Expeditionary Force, and a mob of screaming people leapt out, carrying cameras, microphones, and cages. Milquetoast motioned for silence.

"I've told you all how I captured the monster," said the housebug grandly. "And now, if you'll just spell my name right in the newspapers, he's all yours!"

Then Opus and Ronald-Ann stepped aside to reveal, well, a very unusual beast. Nobody in the crowd noticed, but this basselope had wieners for horns, tomatoes for eyeballs, and two bananas for fangs. To Milquetoast, the monster looked suspiciously like a cat wearing his lunch.

The crowd exploded into a blur of whirring cameras and shouted questions. Milquetoast screamed, "We're being hoodwinked!" but nobody heard. Opus and Ronald-Ann slinked away as the crowd closed in on the beast.

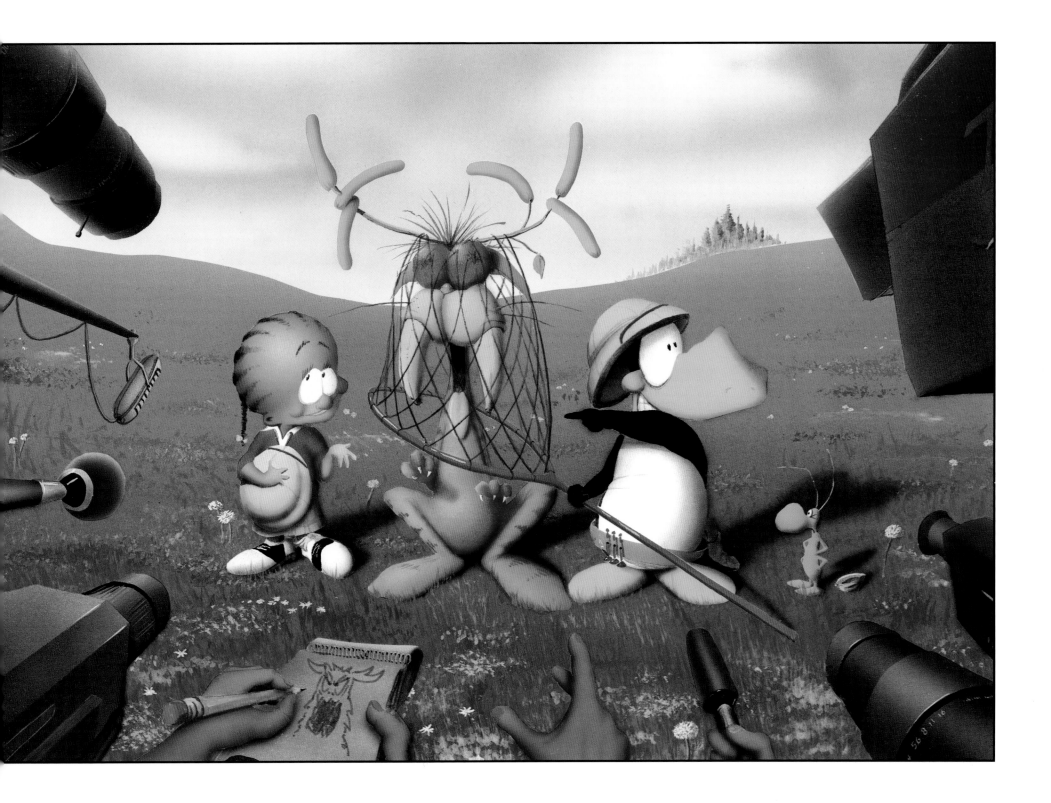

The two reached Rosebud, who was hiding under the pile of dandelions, far away from the shouting crowd. "I think you'd better leave now," Opus told the basselope softly.

Ronald-Ann kissed Rosebud on the nose and slipped him a small spray bottle. "Delighted to have made your acquaintance," she whispered. Rosebud hugged her with his huge ears, and then she ran off to help Bill with the mob.

Opus handed Rosebud a last snack for the road. "A Great and Famous Discoverer knows that some secrets are better left *un*discovered," Opus said sadly.

"Then I have one more undiscovery," said the beast. "Just for you." He scrunched up his eyes, and his face turned pink with strain. Slowly at first and then quickly, his antlers expanded like glowing balloons. They rose above his head, and gently, ever so gently, Rosebud's feet lifted off the ground.

"The stories never mentioned *this*," said a thrilled Opus, laughing and waving good-bye.

A trail of dandelion wisps danced in the last glow of sunlight as Rosebud drifted gracefully toward a deeper, more distant part of the forest. He hoped that ahead might be a quieter place, certainly a less ferocious place.

He looked back at the tiny figure still waving far below, and he smiled. He smiled because it occurred to him that after a very, terribly long time, the World's Last Basselope was actually the World's *First* Basselope With Friends.